Shannon Wedo

Squire the Squirrel and the

Queens Jubilee Celebration

BUMBLEBEE PAPERBACK EDITION

Copyright © Shannon Wedo 2024

The right of Shannon Wedo to be identified as author of this work has been asserted in accordance with sections 77 and 78 of the Copyright, Designs and Patents Act 1988.

All Rights Reserved
No reproduction, copy or transmission of this publication may be made without written permission.
No paragraph of this publication may be reproduced, copied or transmitted save with the written permission of the publisher, or in accordance with the provisions of the Copyright Act 1956 (as amended).
Any person who commits any unauthorised act in relation to this publication may be liable to criminal prosecution and civil claims for damage.
A CIP catalogue record for this title is available from the British Library.

ISBN: 978-1-83934-928-7

Bumblebee Books is an imprint of
Olympia Publishers.

First Published in 2023

Bumblebee Books
Tallis House
2 Tallis Street
London
EC4Y 0AB
Printed in Great Britain
www.olympiapublishers.com

Dedication

I dedicate this book to my three children. Elaynna, my daughter, and my twin sons, Chance and Chase. Each is following their own adventure.

CHAPTER 1

It's a fine April morning to dig up my last treasures of winter! I've hidden my nuts so well; not even the crows that are so adept at ferreting them out of my hiding places can find them. In a few days, I will go to the most important stash vault of all! In the next few months, as the miraculous seasons change and the days linger longer and longer, the trees and flowers will grow heavy with a new bounty for next winter... Now I will enjoy, eat and play during the endless bloom of spring.

Squire the Squirrel darted from tree to tree, greeting all of his posh garden friends – for they were all very aware of how fortunate they all were to have made their homes in the queen's royal garden. They lived in the middle of London. Most of London was tall buildings, motor cars, concrete and the smell of petrol. But here in the royal garden, it was a nature's paradise, tended by the royal gardeners, who were fastidious in the care and upkeep of it all. 1608 was the year King James I established the gardens, with every monarch after, more has been added. Queen Elizabeth II added the extensive rose gardens in the 1960s. The large lake was added in 1828 by Queen Victoria, for 'perch and gudgeon', among other types of fish. There are mulberry trees and hundreds of other varieties. The flowers include over two hundred different varieties! That is a feast for the honey bees that have two hives there. It was all so PERFECT!

He was hopping and digging and concentrating completely on his task, so he was quite startled when

his long-time friend and buddy popped his head out of the gopher hole. One of many throughout the garden, he had an entire city underneath the surface, much to the chagrin of the tireless gardeners. "Good day to you, Squire!" Godfrey said jovially. Squire the Squirrel was so startled he leapt in the air and dropped the entire bounty he had been gathering all morning.

"I REALLY wish you wouldn't do that Godfrey," Squire scoffed, "you could whistle or sing as you approach."

"Sorry Squire, but as you know, I neither whistle nor sing. You should pay attention to your surroundings, young sir. It could have been Roger coming to bully you out of your nuts."

Roger was one of the skulk of red foxes that lived in the garden as well. If you are unsure about what a skulk is, it is the name of a group of foxes. A group is sometimes called a CHARM as well... Our Roger likes to refer to his gang as a SKULK, he thinks it is a fiercesome word. Roger would like to be fiercesome you see, but for now, Roger is scared of his own shadow. He wants very badly to be bold and brave. Hence, he scares the smaller animals for practice.

"Gather your nuts and your wits, Squire. I have exciting news! You must pay attention!"

CHAPTER 2

Squire revelled in exciting news. Hopefully, it was more exciting than last week when the ducklings had started to hatch. Everyone had been so "Over the moon" to see these fuzzy creatures. Daisy and Douglas (the proud parents of the ducklings) had hosted a party and had played a guessing game – everyone had to guess if the next egg to hatch was going to be a girl or boy. The one who guessed correctly got to name the duckling. He hadn't guessed correctly on any of them.

Godfrey settled in beside him at the bottom of the live oak tree. "Squire, do you know what next week is?"

"Is it my birthday? I cannot believe I forgot my own birthday!"

"No," Godfrey the Gopher said. "You did not forget your birthday. It is our queen's seventieth jubilee!"

CHAPTER 3

"Her majesty has been ruling on her throne for seventy years! The longest ruling monarch in HISTORY! Also, may I remind you, Squire, she's the one who ensures that our world, this beautiful garden that all of us call home, is taken care of so meticulously. We owe her a lot."

"I agree," said Squire. "Should we make her a card? She'd like a nice card, I think. We could put glitter on it and cut it into the shape of a crown. We could do that... but I have some more exciting news... the swan family is hosting a big party."

CHAPTER 4

"They are calling it a "SOIRÉE" because it is going to be very fancy. Elizabeth and Phillip – the swans, feel it is their royal duty. After all, they had been named by the royals themselves, Elizabeth and Phillip – after Queen Elizabeth and Prince Phillip.

"It was a ceremony many years ago... Papa swan, Philip now, had fallen in love. Hopelessly and completely in love with Mummy swan, now Elizabeth.

"The real Queen Elizabeth and her Prince Phillip were hosting the first garden party of the season twenty years ago. When Prince Philip saw the young swans together and under the influence of his forever love for his own soul mate Elizabeth, he publicly christened the two young swans, Elizabeth and Philip. Swans also mate for life. Now the swans feel it is their duty as namesakes to host a large garden party of their own for all of the fortunate animals that live in the royal garden," Godfrey the Gopher said.

It was the only thing everyone in the entire garden was talking about! The excitement was like electricity! One could feel it in the air!

CHAPTER 5

Many preparations had to be done to be sure. The location had been decided upon at least. They would have it on the east side of the large lake. Now that, Squire had heard the grand news, he wanted more than anything else to be a part of the preparations.

I could be a big help and make my acorn pie.

His mouth watered just thinking about it. He thanked his buddy Godfrey and off her went, as squirrels do, stopping at every sniff of a treat, tree by tree. He arrived on the shore of the lake to see most of the animals that lived in the garden crowded together, squawking and chirping, squealing, and honking.

What's causing all of the ruckus? Surely not everyone would be selected for preparation duty. He had to get to the edge water, he thought. He could see Elizabeth and Phillip Swan trying desperately to get order queued up. This was his chance to dash to the front. He was young and agile and fast as the wind. Off he went, darting so fast he fell straight into Elizabeth. (Everyone calls her simply Mummy.) Elizabeth, uh, Mummy was so startled she honked and even nipped at Squire.

"My dear Squire! You must never rush into me in that manner! Fore, as beautiful and tranquil swans are known to be, I DO have animal instincts to protect myself. You came dangerously close to losing that fluffy tail you use as your trademark. Now, dear boy, may I ask what is so urgent? Surely you see all of this madness around you. Everyone wants my attention to make sure they can participate in the 'Soirée' for our queen's seventieth jubilee celebration."

Squire had a chance to catch his breath and gather his thoughts. "Dearest Mummy Swan that is precisely why I had to get to the front of the queue. I must be a part of this historic event!"

Mummy Swan clucked and clucked. "Well, of course dear Squire, but you must learn patience and wait your turn. You may have your say when it's your turn. Now to the back of the line my dear one. We shall speak soon." Squire understood. He always knew he was impulsive and quite impatient. Yet, it was part of being a squirrel.

CHAPTER 6

Squire reached the front of the queue. "Finally!" Squire said. "Mummy Swan I have a fabulous idea well, two actually."

"Start with the first one Squire, calm yourself and speak," Mummy Swan said. Squire began.

"You know I have the best recipe for Acorn Pie in the entire garden. I could make my special Acorn pie in fact I may need to make several pies. Which brings me to my second suggestion," he said excitedly.

"One moment Squire, one idea at a time my boy. Let's discuss these mouth-watering pies of yours. I must say, I absolutely love your acorn pie. Yes you will need to make many, many pies. Everyone will be there. You may want to start right away!"

"Oh Mummy! I will! It will be so much fun! Now, can we talk about my second idea?"

"Yes, Squire, I am listening."

"My skill and agility would allow me to deliver them too, and very fast!"

"Oh, my dear Squire, I do love your enthusiasm. I assure you, you are going to be so busy with gathering the acorns and other ingredients for your pies there will be no time for another task.

"Elaynna, the red fox and her three daughters from the charm of fox, have volunteered for the job of writing out invitations... That is a job they have already started today. Mitilda, Harriett and Lucinda, the three old crows are coming out of retirement to do the deliveries. This will give them a chance to

be helpful as well. They spend too much time up by the street lights gossiping anyway. In fact, dear boy, your pies may require you to get some help from some of the other animals. This is a big job and an even bigger responsibility. You concentrate on that, Squire."

CHAPTER 7

Squire scurried off again, the way squirrels do, this time with a mission. As he stopped tree by tree, he gathered the acorns now. After the second tree, he found he wouldn't be able to carry them all back to his own oak tree alone. He took what he could carry and went home to think about who he would ask to assist him on this very important task. He made it through his door and dropped the armful of acorns on the table.

First thing, I will make myself a nice cup of cream tea, he thought.

Tea always helps me think better.

He put the kettle on and got the porcelain teapot from the china cabinet. His mind was going through the list of friends he could choose from to help. Of course, Godfrey the Gopher, after all, Godfrey was his best friend. Godfrey's brother, Alfie, he'd feel left out if he didn't ask him. Then there was Henrietta the White Hare and her siblings…

Oh gosh! She must have ten siblings! All of them would never fit inside his tree house! What about the Robin family that had their nest up on the branch of the same oak tree he lived in? They would have their feelings hurt if he didn't ask them. He made a cup of tea and sat down. He had no idea this was going to be such a big decision. Then he thought of Charlie, Chance and Chase; the chipmunks. Now his mind was spinning! What about his beautiful Butterfly friends, Ava and Aria? For sure, he had to include them in some way. He sipped his tea and tried to calm his racing mind. He was so tired from all of the day's activities he fell asleep even before he had finished his tea. While he slept, he was restless, in his mind were the faces of all of his friends. Some were tearful, some were angry, some were blank and quiet. He woke up suddenly with his heart pounding. He knew where to go for advice. It was a perfect time too. It was one o'clock in the morning. They would be wide awake by now. Yes! They would give him the best advice.

CHAPTER 8

He heated the leftover tea, gulped it down, threw on his velvet jacket and into the deep woods he went. He was going to visit the parliament. The five very old, very wise owls. They were the parliament of owls that everyone went to seek out their sage advice. The wisest in the gardens, everyone agreed.

He arrived deep in the forest where the parliament of owls lived. It was kind of spooky. He could hear the wind whistling through the tree branches. Then he heard Grandpapa Owl, "Whoo! Whoo! Who goes there? I demand you reveal yourself at once!"

Squire stood at attention and meekly spoke, "It is I sir, Squire the Squirrel from the other side of the garden."

"State your purpose – you must have one to show up here without an appointment! We have rules you know, our society would be chaos without following the rules!"

He then heard Grandmama speak, "Grandpapa, be easy on Squire, he is but a young squirrel – he will learn the ways of society soon enough. My instincts tell me he needs guidance and he needs it immediately!"

CHAPTER 9

There were five owls in this parliament, all of them were family. Grandpapa, Grandmama, Da, Ma, and Dudley. In that order.

"Yes, yes, dear boy, do get on with it then – what is your question? But I warn you, it better not be 'how many licks does it take to get to the centre of a tootsie roll pop? That stopped being funny years ago!'"

Squire cleared his throat and explained his big responsibility of making his acorn pies for the queen's seventieth year jubilee celebration. Yet when he started gathering the ingredients, he realized he needed help. His dilemma was he had so many friends he didn't know how to choose who to do what job or anything about organizing a group. He was feeling overwhelmed. He even thought it was too big a responsibility and maybe he should just tell mummy swan, he could not do it. His lips began to tremble, and his eyes weld with tears. He was overcome with emotion and cried. All he ever wanted was to be part of the celebration.

The entire parliament flew down beside him, patted his back and wiped his tears away with their wings.

"There, there my boy... Everything will work out. We will guide you. We will help you make a plan."

"Yes! Yes!" said Ma. "It only takes a bit of organizing. You have many parts to organize. Don't get ahead of yourself. You already showed initiative seeking out our help. This is how you learn."

"Of course, Squire. Quite right my boy," Da agreed. He flew to the inside of the knobby tree then returned with pen and paper.

"First the list. Think Squire, what do you need first?"

Squire thought for a moment, then said, "Well, I need to gather all of the ingredients for the pies."

"Correct my boy. Now you understand!" Da exclaimed. "That's a perfect place to start. Do you know anyone who would be good at that task?"

Squire immediately answered yes, his best friend Godfrey and his brother Alfie. They are the gopher brothers and have underground passageways to get it all back to his kitchen quickly. Then there's Chance, Chase and Charlie. They are chipmunks who are strong and good at balancing a lot of nuts at once. Now Squire was getting excited! Then there's Henrietta…

"Whoa, whoa, whoa!" said Grandpapa. "You are getting ahead of yourself again Squire, THINK, with you and the chaps you already named, how many is that?"

Squire thought for a moment. "Let's see, Godfrey, Alfie, Chance, Chase, Charlie and myself. That's a total of six gatherers."

Grandmama broke in, "With six gatherers, you could gather all of the ingredients you need in two hours. That would be plenty of time. Many hands make light work! Remember that Squire."

Ma then asked what the next task would be. Squire tapped his foot, thinking hard, then he exclaimed, "It's time to bake the pies!"

Ma smiled patiently and said, "Almost, but something has to be done BEFORE you start baking. What do you normally do Squire?"

THINK! He tapped his chin with his finger then said, "I know! I have to prepare all of the ingredients in the kitchen, which includes washing them, cracking and chopping the nuts and preparing the pie crust. Oh yes! All of that must be done before cooking!"

"Right you are!" Dudley Owl piped in.

"Do you know of anyone who might be good at the food prep stage?"

"Yes I do! Henrietta the Hare and her siblings. They do everything fast. After all, they are cousins to the rabbits. But there are so many of them. They would never all fit in my tiny kitchen."

"Think about the size of your kitchen. How many do you think would fit?" Dudley asked.

Squire thought, then decided on four. "Yes. Four would fit, but what about the other seven?"

"Boy, they would be awfully disappointed."

Grandpapa spoke then. "When I was with the royal air force, we fed so many we lined up tables around the trees in the forest – perhaps you could set up tables outside your tree house and the brothers and sisters could use those. There's plenty of room outside your tree."

Squire's eyes lit up. "That's brilliant sir! Why didn't I think of that?"

"Awe my boy, because, you see, I am the WISE OLD OWL... NOT you!"

CHAPTER 10

To the next task Squire! Much to organize still! Squire agreed. Now would be the time to cook the pies. This would be where he would shine! He and his best friend Godfrey the Gopher, just the two of them cooking in the kitchen.

Twenty acorn pies. Ten each. After the pies bake, we can sit them on the cleaned tables outside to cool. That would give his lovely butterfly friends, Ava and Aria, their opportunity to help. Their task would be to place the empty acorn tops in the centre of the pies and wrap the edges in a fine honey roping to complete the decoration on the pies. The finishing touches only the lightness of a butterfly could perfect. Everything was coming together wonderfully now. The only task left would be transporting the twenty pies to the site of the jubilee celebration by the lake.

Chase, Chance and Charlie, the chipmunks would load the pies on the wagon carefully, four pies per wagon. Squire was having difficulty figuring out how many wagons would be needed. Grandpapa suggested simple math.

"Listen, lad, you have room in each wagon for four pies – five wagons with four pies in each equals twenty pies."

Then Ma Owl told Squire to take his list and go home while he still had a few hours to sleep. He would wake refreshed and ready to contact his friends.

"You have all you need from us, lad. Off you go, we will see you tomorrow night at the party to be sure. It will be a delicious feast!" Pa Owl said.

Squire said good bye and scurried home with his organized list tucked safely in his pocket.

CHAPTER 11

He slept until he heard the birds sing at dawn. The big seventieth year jubilee celebration is today! He scurried up the oak tree to ask the robin family if they would fly through the garden to tell all of his friends he had come up with a plan and to meet at his tree house and the time each group should arrive. The robins tweeted and twirled! They appreciated being included too. Off they flew.

The first to arrive was his best friend, Godfrey and his brother, Alfie. Then the chipmunks, Chance, Chase, and Charlie, including Squire, there were six gatherers. Each of them went off on their own to forage for ingredients to make the pies. In an hour, they had all of the ingredients and all of the acorns they needed. The gophers and the chipmunks dropped their goodies in the kitchen at Squire's tree house.

"Ta, see you at the lake later!" They all said. Now his friends were arriving to help prepare the ingredients.

Henrietta the Hare and her many siblings came hopping up the path. Squire was very happy to see all of them. They each took to their task, setting up the prep tables outside, arranging the bowls, chopping blocks, pans, and plates. Utensils for cutting and large bowls of water for cleaning.

Henrietta, the oldest sibling, already possessed good organizing skills. She had helped with all of her younger brothers and sisters since they were born. The younger siblings listened to her instructions

carefully before starting their work.

Henrietta always said, "Many hands make light work." That was her favourite quote. She liked it so much that she had it embroidered on her work apron. She was very proud of her hare family. In practically no time, all of the hares' work was complete. They returned home to "Dress to impress" at the party. Squire waved goodbye to all of them, promising to see them late at the lake.

Just then, Godfrey raced in the door, anxious and excited to get started baking the pies. Squire was busy mixing and blending, sneaking a taste of this, added spice to that, when he exclaimed, "Oh, how fun this all is!"

"No one will ever forget this celebration. It's going to be the biggest I have ever attended."

Godfrey agreed as he dipped his finger in the pie.

In a few minutes, the delicious scent floated in the wind through the entire garden. The last pie came out of the oven. Squire was finished. He and Godfrey had the honour of licking the bowls. What a treat, indeed!

CHAPTER 12

Godfrey went home to get ready for the party… "Soirée" as everyone was calling it. It must be pretty fancy, he had never been to a soirée before. He wanted to look smart in his new jacket and hat he had only worn once before at his auntie Kate's wedding.

While the pies sat on the tables cooling, Ava and Aria, the beautiful butterfly sisters, arrived. Squire sat back and relaxed against his tree, talking with Ava and Aria while he took a break. He was feeling so good about all of his friends chipping in to help him make his pies a success. Ava and Aria understood how he felt. Having friends and family in your life makes everything you do, everything you see, indeed, everything you experience even more special. Your memories are made with the people you choose to let into your life.

The pies had cooled completely now. Ava and Aria set to decorating them with ease and care only butterflies possess. In a short time, the task was completed.

"How absolutely beautiful they look, lasses! I must take photographs with my camera to remember these special pies and this special celebration always!" Squire exclaimed.

Ava and Aria thought that was a splendid idea. Time was getting short, so they flitted away to get themselves ready for the soirée.

"Ta Ta, see you by the lake soon!" said the Butterfly sisters.

Squire washed his hands and face, put on his special jacket and hat, and waited for Chance, Chase and Charlie to arrive to load the pies in the five red wagons. Just enough room for four pies in each wagon. The chipmunks arrived and loaded the pies with care. What a spectacle they all would make, approaching the lake together – Squire in the front, followed by Chance, Chase and Charlie; the chipmunks, ended the procession with four red foxes to ensure no vultures or wild beast dare to dodge off with a pie or two before they arrived at the main celebration by the lake. They walked the winding path through the beautiful garden. They passed many of his friends' homes along the way. The animals were waving and cheering to Squire and his entourage. He had never felt such pride and love before. This was a joyful day, indeed.

CHAPTER 13

They could hear the musicians playing their instruments as they came around the magnificent rose garden. The excitement was electrifying! There at the water's edge were Elizabeth and Phillip Swan – the regal swan family waiting to congratulate Squire. All of the animals of the garden now quietly watching him, Squire became a bit shy. He had never had all of the attention focused on him before. His chipmunk friends pulled the wagons full of the acorn pies in front of the swans and stepped back. The red foxes, having completed their duty, stepped aside. The royal swans stepped up to inspect the acorn pies. Squire was holding his breath in anticipation.

Would they approve? Were the pies up to jubilee standard?

Mummy Swan took a beautiful ornate silver knife and fork and cut a small, delicate slice of pie. Squire felt like time had frozen at that moment. Just when he thought he would burst with anticipation.

Mummy Swan raised her elegant wings and declared for all to hear, "Squires acorn pies are, from this point forward, the official jubilee pies of the kingdom!"

CHAPTER 14

All of the animals, birds and beasts clapped, clucked, tweeted and cheered. The pies were sliced and passed around for everyone at the garden party to enjoy. This day had been the highlight of Squire the Squirrel's life. He thanked the regal swans and everyone for helping make his pies a big success. Then with his own plate of pie and a fork, he joined his friends and relaxed by the red wagons, enjoying his now famous acorn pie.

About the Author

Shannon lives and writes on the Chesapeake Bay in Norfolk, Virginia U.S.A. She still finds time to travel the globe, creating adventures of her own that may one day find its way onto the page.

Acknowledgements

Thank you to my granddaughters Ava and Aria for all the nighttime wanderings on the Chesapeake Bay,

Printed in the USA
CPSIA information can be obtained
at www.ICGtesting.com
CBHW040855310824

13887CB00002B/6